secrets to
the
art
of
trickin'

A'Lisa Ray & Thee Stallion

DEDICATION

To all those out here trickin'--trick,
and to all those who have been tricked,
those getting tricked right now,
and those who will be tricked in the future.
May you not lose everything in this trickin' game.

CONTENTS

ACKNOWLEDGMENTS

Thank all the tricks who got over on you and made you stronger.
This book contains the secrets to the art of trickin'. It is a manual for
the tricks and a guide for those who will be victims of the trickery.

1
TRICKIN'—IT IS AN ART

Trickin' is one of Earth's oldest institutions, not prostitution but trickin'. Eve was in the Garden of Eden trickin'—she was not a prostitute, and she was not out there whoring—she was trickin'. The sly, slippery snake, "the Devil—old Satan himself," should not have even had a chance to spit his game. The moment, he said, "Hey Bae, let me talk to you," Eve should have replied, "I got a man, and we ain't got nothing to talk about." Eve had a good man—a God-fearing man. But she wanted something that her man wasn't providing—that damn apple. Her "love of material things" led her to entertain the snake, not because she wanted a relationship with the snake or because Adam was doing a horrible job providing for her in the garden but because she had a materialistic nature. She entertained the snake because she wanted something beyond her means—something that she did not even need. Because of that need, she had to run even more game on her man Adam so that he would go along with her plan. Trickin' began in the Garden of Eden. It existed with the beginning of man. As long as man has been on earth, trickin' has been in the equation.

This book is about the art of trickin'. We give no judgement on whether trickin' is right or wrong, or good or bad. Trickin' has been here since man's existence and will stay here until the last human perishes. We simply want you to be able to recognize it when it happens. Toward that goal, this is a manual and a guide on trickin'. Its major aim is to help individuals—particularly men—know when they are being tricked. Tricks can be both men and women; however, this book is written from the perspective of the trick being a woman. To my lady tricks, please forgive me for exposing the secrets but it is time that we give help and assistance to some of the simps, pimps, players, and lovers. There are some good men out here who are being tricked and played with unnecessarily—they deserve better. If only they would read this phenomenal work of literature as we already know if you want to keep a secret, just hide it in a book. In this edition, we give light to men who are in the darkness and who are playing lead actor in their own delusion before it's too late.

A good trick will make you believe that she loves you and have no problem telling you that she loves you. Love is the greatest asset in the trickin' game, so do like the Bible says and "guard your hearts" because a trick, like Cupid, will put an arrow through your heart.

Tricks have gone by various names across the eons—gold-diggers, hoes, hoochies, skanks, tramps—those who are in the relationship for something other than real, genuine, true love. Many of our mothers may have been tricks. Tricks are in the situation for their benefit—usually a financial benefit which is why terms like "gold digger" have been applied. Securing the bag is often the main objective but shelter, living provisions, getting hair and nails done, clothes, groceries, cars are equally desirable goods. Yes, there are ladies out here trickin' just to get their hair and nails done. High maintenance women are notorious for the trickin' lifestyle. They place conditions on being in a relationship—if you are my man, then you must pay for my hair appointment or nail appointment. Guys who are natural providers will easily be inclined to fulfill these desires, even if done grudgingly. It's just something that they would do for anyone they loved and felt obliged to take care of.

John Witherspoon, the late great comedian, once responded to the question, "How can I tell if my girl is hoochie?". He laughingly remarked, "Call them what you want but in 1962 they were hoes. They know who they are. They brand themselves. Tattoos on their lower back—like a tramp stamp, tattoos on their arm, up their damn neck, tattoos down their leg. That's the key to tell you that I am a hoe—I sells pussy. 25 earrings in your ear, titties full of earrings. What are you going to do, put some keys on that motherf@cker. If she go to work at 9 and come home at 3 a.m. in the morning talking about she a secretary—yea right, you are a secretary on that pole....She can lie and say that she ain't no hoochie—I went to Harvard. So, you are a Harvard hoe—don't try to be nothing else. This is America, you can be anything you want." For comedic purposes, I wanted to illustrate the differences and subtle nuances of how we define trickin'. In the 1960s and 1970s, "trick" was slang for engaging in a sexual act for money. For example, "turn a trick" implies that you had sex for money. In the evolution of the term, trickin' is about more than sex in most cases but certainly about financial or material gain. Trickin' has gotten sophisticated as women have learned how not to have sex and still get what they want. As a result, the trick plays the man for her benefit by cunningly and convincingly treating him like he is in a loving relationship. In some cases, all the woman has to do is show some genuine concern—not even to the level of love.

Tricks can come in all shapes, sizes and ages—there are young tricks and old seasoned tricks. The category doesn't matter, they usually have the same mission—to secure the bag or whatever their need may be. Tricks are master strategists, almost borderline narcissistic but so very dangerous if the trick you fall in love with lacks emotional intelligence or lacks emotional concern for your well-being.

The trickin' game has evolved given the presence of

technology and the expansive use of social media platforms to find new marks and victims. It is a dangerous game for the good guy out here.

We want to take just a moment properly framing the current definition of trickin'. We are aware that trickin' can still be used interchangeably with "hoeing," "whoring," or "gold-digging". It is a noun and a verb. It describes both a person and an action. A trick is one who tricks and engages in trickin'. Over the next few chapters, we will expound, explore, and explain the art of trickin' in through the lens of a 2025 perspective.

2
THE BAG

"Girl, get your bag!" is the mantra for all those who trick. If you have ever said it, then you are a trick. If another woman has ever said it to you, then you are probably perceived as a trick. Just as "game" recognizes "game," tricks recognize tricks. Tricks around the world are driven and motivated to "get the bag"—money bag, shelter bag, purse bag, clothing bag, jewelry bag, daycare bag, light bill bag, rent bag, new car bag. The bag is a metaphor for whatever the benefit the trick is receiving out of the trickin' relationship—this is a paid internship, and the man usually is the last one to realize it.

Securing the bag usually requires a set of calculated, strategized, and well-organized power plays, especially if the woman is trickin' with more than one man. Trickin'—good trickin' requires skill particularly if you are trying to offer more than pussy or if your mark (male victim) has emotional needs that require daily or regular engagement.

Men should understand that they have the bag, and the trick wants what he can provide. His usefulness is only as good as the bag. The problem is a lot of men—particularly the good men, will fall in love with the trick. Love will then cause him to lose his mind and his wallet. An old term that we will discuss in another chapter is "simping". A simp is a man who falls head over heels in love with his woman and showers her with gifts and anything else that she asks for without the ability to say,

"No". Another way of saying this for the old folk is "hen-pecked" or "pussy-whipped". Either way, a man—a provider—will attempt to meet the needs of his woman if he is truly in love with her. He will make sure that she gets her bag and even more if he loves her. The trick will do what she can to make sure that the mark believes that she loves him as much as he loves her. Men, you cannot fall in love too soon! You need to make sure that the love is real before you open your bank account, wallets, and pockets. You will only have yourself to blame in the end when you are broke and heart-broken because the trick has left you for another mark.

In addition to guarding your heart, you need to guard your bank account. You are not an ATM machine or her personal financial institution. But on the only hand, that is exactly what you—her personal bank. Begin watch what happens when you say, "No" or "I don't got it." If you notice a bad attitude, a tantrum, or distance then take those signs as red flags. We will talk more about those red flags in another chapter.

The trick is only in this situation for the bag. Sometimes it may start out with the hope for love, but things will change, and the trick only remains invested for the purpose of securing the bag. The change may not have anything to do with the man, but everything to do with a change in her personal financial situation. Men you must be able to adapt and walk away. Walking away or terminating the relationship can be one of the hardest things that you do, especially if you really love her. This is the woman of your life, the love of your life—you don't want anyone but her; however, she only wants the bag. Do not get this twisted—it's all about the bag.

The question to men is: how much is the bag worth to you? Is it worth your self-dignity? Is it worth being disrespected? It is worth compromising your love values and settling for less because you have fallen in love with someone that is in the relationship for your provisions and not your personality. This is a quid pro quo type of relationship—you do for me, and I will do for you. And in order to keep me doing, then you certainly have to do what I ask you to do. Trickin' has gotten very sophisticated because of CashApp, PayPal, Venmo, Zelle, direct deposit—all these apps that allow money transfer to happen virtually. Cash no longer needs to exchange hands. Mr. Charlie does not have to leave money on the nightstand before he exits. You don't even have to see Mr. Charlie for him to make your CashApp bling or your Zelle ring. Groceries no longer require going to the grocery store. You can use online delivery sites that will professionally have those items placed at the tricks doorstep without you laying one eye or one finger or any other part on her. As the game evolves, so with the methods used to gain access to the bag. But no matter how much things change, the aim of making believe they love you as much as you love them is still the essence of trick behavior. Follow the bag, and you will see how much you are valued, appreciated, or respected.

3
HOW TO SPOT THE TRICK

Spotting a trick can be a difficult challenge, especially if you love the woman. The last thing you want to believe is that the person that you are madly in love with, does not really want you. A good trick will play the game so well, that it will be hard to recognize that game. But your gut and intuition will tell you. If you are always insecure about something or second guessing some behavior, then you are probably right. A woman who is truly into you would try to her best to minimize or eliminate behaviors that triggered your feelings of doubt or insecurity. Now at that same time, if you are a man, then you need to be a man. Try to get out of your feelings (men have feelings) and see objectively what is going on. And if the lady is immature or emotionally unavailable and does not want to talk about your issues of concern, then that is a red flag, and you know that you are probably dealing with a trick!

In Chapter 1, I shared with you a comical skit by John Witherspoon where he shared how to spot a hoochie. But he was right when he said that "hoochies brand themselves". Tricks brand themselves too, not just with tattoos but with literal brands—FashionNova, Shein, Gucci, Chanel, Lululemon—all of them. Most tricks have an aura of high maintenance. Their Instagram profiles scream high maintenance—ass out, titties out, tattoos, wigs with long inches, fake nails, lashes, and super tight or little to no clothes to accentuate sexual body parts. This is branding, marketing, and advertising all rolled up into one. You will find her in the club smoking hookah and taking shots of Don Julio or some wretched liver-killing paint remover being sold as alcoholic liquor. If the wig is blonde, and she is not a White girl—you have just spotted a trick. If she is twerking on a chair or section in the makeshift VIP section, trick! Approach is your own risk and in other words, buyer beware. You are getting exactly what you seek—heartbreak, misery, and a toxic relationship. You will be played to the utmost if you believe that this woman is going to love you like the 30-year relationship you saw Big Ma and Grandpa in—not to say that grandma wasn't tricking but that love stood the test of time even if through necessity. They were getting into clubs during their teenage years with fake ids. They are skilled at trickin'.

Simply put, some tricks you can see coming from a mile away. If you ask a woman out on a date and she replies, "If you want to go out with me, then I am going to need you to do my hair or nails,"—no doubt that is a trick. The relationship starts off transactional at best. Another is: "If you want to go out with me, then CashApp me to let me know that you are serious." You got to be out of your mind if you want a man to pay you to POSSIBLY show up to a meal that he should be paying for any way since he asked you out. It does not make sense. And men, if you agree to these stipulations prior to the date, then you are setting yourself up to be tricked and deserve exactly what you get. The outcome will not be in your favor. Women who are too good for the Cheesecake Factory are too good for your bag— keep it moving. A good woman, although not ideal, will eat with in you in the park. A picnic will be sufficient for a good woman. Some things can be avoided, and some people can be avoided—so use common sense. Do not be blinded by how pretty or good looking you think a woman may be or how warm and wet you find her pussy. Do not settle for a 10 in the face with 0 in empathy or emotional intelligence. You will pay twice, double, and dearly for those dangerous combinations.

These tricks are more advanced with their game than most men are capable of spotting. This is why the game is so easy with most tricks. Men make it easy. The trick learns what you want, gives it to you, and then raises the price. If you want to keep it, you are going to have to pay more and more for it. This is just how the game works. Tricks get raises too. And usually, you are too far in, too deep in love, and too comfortable that you don't want to see your good thing end. (Blues song on the speaker: Please don't let a good thing enddddd! Because it hurts too much to start all over againnn!)

The highest-level trick is the one that is unrecognizable. She looks like a good wholesome woman—someone that you could actually bring home to your mother, someone that you could actually make a baby with—God knows that would be a horrible decision. She will even seem sweet, intelligent, and is beautiful. However, she is just saying the "right" thing to achieve her bag.

Below are a few signs that you might be dealing with a trick:

- If she carries two phones, then she might be a trick. Why do you need two phones. The president of the United States doesn't need two phones.

- If the phone goes on "do not disturb" or "notifications have been silenced" then you likely dealing with a trick.

- If she carries her phoneS with her into the bathroom, then you are dealing with a trick.

- If she turns her location off, then you are dealing with a trick. Giving someone your location should not be a big deal if you feel safe. Naturally, he will want your location if he cares about your protection and believes that you are his woman. If she doesn't give you the location or makes a big deal about the location sharing, then she is a trick. Just because the location says that you are home doesn't mean that you are actually there. As a trick, you want to do everything that you can to build his trust.

- If she stops answering her phone after a certain hour, then she is a trick. You will hear that "I feel asleep". I'm sure that you did fall asleep, right after Tyrone dicked you down. Tyrone is listening to the phone ring when you call.

- If she removes you from being able to see her Instagram story, then she is a trick. Just run away. For what reason would you prohibit someone, especially the one you supposed to love, from watching your Instagram stories. If a man stays after he has been removed from being able to see the IG story, then he knows he is a mark and is just waiting to see how long this situation will last. He just hasn't found his feet to exit. But the moment he stops trying to be added back to view, he is already aware that this ship is sinking.

- If she never introduces you to her friends or family, you are getting tricked.

- If she crashes out about you staying over at her place, then you are getting tricked.

- If she doesn't tell men that approach her that she is not single and in relationship, then she is a trick! Remember Eve and the Devil. She should have shut the Devil down the moment he spoke because she had a man.

- If you here these words: "Would you be interested in buying me..." or "Would you like to make a contribution to ...," you are dealing with a trick.

23

4
DO'S AN DON'TS OF TRICKIN'

There are some basic do's and don'ts of trickin'.

First some basic advice to the tricks—once your mark loses trust in you, he will think that you are a cheater. Do all that you can to keep your mark in the dark about your cheating and treacherous ways. Keep your lies simple because eventually your story will need to add up.

DO'S FOR THE TRICK

- **Be consistent:** These young marks will often ask for a good morning text. Once you start, this will be your normal pattern. Now of course when you wake up, you are going to copy and paste, "Good morning," to all of your marks. This can be done at the same time. You can even ask Siri to send the texts for you. Simply speak: Send separate good morning text to clown#1 and clown#2. Done. Move on with your day. Once you miss a day, the mark will believe that something is off and that you are cheating. If you call everyday around the same time, this too will become an expected norm and any deviation from this pattern will be viewed as though you are cheating. Don't start what you cannot finish, otherwise you create more hassle for yourself.

- **Pick a mark with a small number of**

followers on social media. If you find your mark on social media, make sure that the circle is small and separate from yours. Younger women will of course go for more established older men with stable finances. A young woman want cash without complaints. She has no expectation that a young struggling peer will be able to provide for her needs. A hoe will take the younger guy for dick but not for a long-term partner. So younger guys, if that's you just realize that all you are providing is dick and she is not your girlfriend. She will be loyal to her paycheck. You are just a company keeper, a companion of sorts but she does not belong to you.

- **Do communicate.** Communication is a

critical component to trickin'. You want to communicate with peace and not chaos. Talk through your problems—and there will be problems because the trick is going to cause problems because of her unexplainable inconsistencies.

- **Do be his peace.** Do be the calm in your mark's life. Chaos and stress will only cause confusion, and your mark will begin to question your worth. No man wants to exist in chaos—that's for the birds, fly away with that.

- **Do build trust.** Trust is central to your trickin'. The mark must trust you in order to fall in love deeply. Once he trusts you, you will have everything you want. A man that trusts you will provide you with whatever you ask and is in his ability to provide. A simp— yes but he will voluntarily be your simp if he feels that you are trustworthy, loyal, and committed to him alone. This is the story that you must sell if you want to keep him. No man is cool with another man fucking his main piece. If you sell the idea of mutual love and attraction, then you will get more without even having to ask.

DON'TS FOR THE TRICK

- **Don't ever slip and mention your other mark in front of your main mark.** Your main mark is under the delusion that you are his and belong only to him. Don't do anything that will destroy this delusion and cause the main mark to question your fidelity and faithfulness.

- **Don't flaunt the fact that your other mark flew you out for the weekend.** Your main mark knows that you don't have the money to afford an airplane ticket. Therefore, if you are flying somewhere, then someone else bought that ticket. C'mon before real—no reason believes that you are going to visit your family for the weekend. Your other mark flew you out and all your main mark is thinking about is you taking back shots and sucking dick.

- **Don't disrespect your main mark.** Respect is a major part of the trickin' game. Sure you are using this poor man for his money and his resources—he has to work hard at a job to earn money to support you. He is giving his pay toward your lifestyle. The least you can do is give the man some respect. Do not disrespect your mark. They say there is "no honor among thieves". Well at least have some respect. This is also akin to the advice: "don't bite the hand that feeds you".

- Don't mention your ex. Just don't do it. We all know that you and the ex are probably still fucking on occasion but do not mention him.

DO'S FOR THE MARK

- **Do guard your heart.** This is hard to because most men do want to be in a monogamous relationship where they can trust their partner, even if they aren't married or have desire to marry. Once the mark falls in love, the trick has won her game. She can have anything that she wants at this point—he is a walking ATM machine and will live and breathe to fulfill your every wish.

- **Request her location.** Even if you don't ever check her location, ask for it. Her response and actions only provide you with more information to support her trickery.

- **Make sure that your trick is on a budget.** If you do not provide a budget, she will spend your very last penny.

- **Do collect on every pussy payment.** Make sure that you collect your pussy payments. Don't miss a single payment. Any time that pussy is made available, accept it because you earned it. You will regret missing a payment if the trick decides to be stingy with the pussy or make you wait because she let some other mark have his chance at clapping the cheeks.

- **Do establish regular visiting, especially for the long mark.** Long distance relationships are hard enough when two people really love each other. You must realize that in a long-distance relationship with a trick, there is nothing you can do to keep her attention, loyalty, and faithfulness. She will cry that she needed companionship over your commitment to provide for her lifestyle. You are just a means to an end. Remember that! If you are in a long-distance situation, make sure that you have a bi-weekly visiting schedule at the least. 30 days is too long, and too many factors can occur that can cause this situation to become

unstable. These factors only increase your

anxiety and doubt and worry.

DON'TS FOR THE MARK

- Don't give that trick all your money. These

  old men will give these young girls their

  entire social security check. Do NOT give

  these tricks your absolute last. I guarantee

  that they would not do the same for you.

  You will end up in the poor house with a

  credit score down in the 400s because you

  put everything on the line for the trick.

- Don't put all your eggs in one basket. As

  much as you want this trick to your only

  piece, you are not her only piece. So it is best

to have more than one lover in this regard.

If would be nice to have one lover—one

person that you could trust and have your

back but if you like the tricks then a Proverbs

31 woman is not what you are going to get.

- Don't be afraid to walk away. Man I know it

  will hurt like crazy and that you will grieve

  like somebody died but walking away should

  always be an option. It sounds easier than it

  actually is because you love this trick. This

  trick has become a part of your life, but this

  trick does not ultimately mean you any good.

  It is better to walk away broken than to keep

  going and end up broke. What will happen

  when your money runs out, and it will?

  When your money is gone, the trick is gone.

She does not belong to you, it's just your

turn—however long that will be, and

however much is in your bank account.

5
SIMPS, PIMPS, PLAYERS AND LOVERS: KNOW THYSELF

Shakespeare was on to something when he said, "To thine own self, be true".

You have to know yourself and who you are. The more secure and comfortable you are with yourself, the better the trickin' situation will be. Because at some point, you will have to realize who you are. You will have to remember who you are. You are a catch. Someone on this earth will love the hell out of you. Someone would love to have a committed and dedicated partner like you. Someone would love to give back to you all the love that you give. You are a hardworking man—you get up every day and go to work to earn an honest living for yourself and the ones that you love—that's a good man. Always remember that you are a good man, and you deserve good love where you are treated with respect and emotional care. Do you know how good it is to have someone who cares about whether you ate something today, or is concerned about whether you make it home safely? Emotional intelligence is very important in a relationship. Some people just don't have emotional intelligence, and most tricks don't care enough to develop it because they really don't care about the mark, they only care about what the mark can do for them

. So knowing who you is one of the most important things you can do to save yourself as a mark. Back in the day, the question would be, "Are you a simp or a pimp?". Marks are often considered simps by other men. A simp is someone who gives his lady everything she desires just because he has fallen so deep in love. Men who have mastered not being a simp that the trick is does not belong to the mark and that she is out here doing the same thing to someone else—using folk until she gets her bag secured. Men who understand this are not really to give lavish gifts or empty their wallets knowing that they are dealing with a trick. Tricks who meet resistance from men who recognize their game quickly move on to the next mark. The trick realizes that their bag will be limited and push onward to more fertile ground. Simps are blinded by love—they cannot see the trick for who she is because the wants them to believe that the trick is the best thing on earth—the power of her pussy has whipped him into submission in most cases. The mark does not want to lose his "for sure thing" to lonely nights. He has already invested so much that he feels attached to his investment.

In contrast, pimps and players were men who had whipped the pussy. Pimps were in charge of the pussy and did not let any trickery come his way. Matter of fact, the pimp was a male version of a trick. Pimps are protective but not intoxicated from the vapors of love. Players tended to love the art of romance and achieving the conquest of pulling more than one woman. Players could be heartless in some cases as well because they too were selling dreams of love and exclusive relationships. Last but not least, a lover was one who exhibited some great level of care and concern about his woman. He had no intention to hurt the lady or leave her dry. His goal was to respect her and treat her right.

Men should understand their love language and their love needs. These categories also determine how likely a man is to fall victim to trick. These categories also determine the likelihood that a mark will get taken for all he has. Once you know yourself, you can also begin to set boundaries for what you want, what you don't want, and what you are willing to accept. When you know your worth, you will tolerate the blatant game-playing and disrespect in your face. When you know who you are, walking away becomes a little bit easier because you know something better will eventually come along. Once you realize who you are, then you will be able to call out the bullshit and flip the tables. Instead of the trick having the upper hand, you will have the upper hand because you realize that you were the catch all along. Those groceries didn't arrive on her doorstep without you, those flowers didn't arrive without you, those electronic cash deposits didn't arrive without you and your bank account. You were a critical piece the trickery. Know your role and understand that you are a gift—if not for her, someone out there will love you and treat you that way that you desire to be cared for and loved. If you don't love yourself, you will be stuck chasing people who don't love you either. Refuse to settle for less than what you know is the basic minimum for a loving relationship. Sir, you are a rare breed, quit acting like you are regular. They don't make natural providers and protectors like they used to, but you have to be wise to guard against usuary, deception, and trickery.

6
YOUR OPTIONS

Marks have a few options in these situations: stay or go, expose or let ride, and boss up or continue the status quo.

You have the option of staying in the situation or leaving. If you choose to stay in the situation believing or knowing that you are being tricked is all on you. You should at that point take full responsibility for the stress, mental health decline, and toxicity that is about follow. If you stay, then you accept the deceit and willful trickery to use you to provide her needs. You sign up, almost volunteer to be a simp or a sucker for her cause—which is always "getting the bag".

The moment you decide to stop providing or stop being used, then you are no longer relevant to her mission. You are expendable and you will notice that everything about the situation will become chaotic and inconsistent. You might as well leave the situation at this point because now the only way to make things better is for you to pay double. You will have to work overtime to get back into rhythm and good graces with the trick. An interruption to her bag-getting mission, only gives space for her to entertain and explore other marks. This will further lead to the erosion of your trust and will only serve to increase your level of insecurity. You will begin to second-guess everything—is she really visiting family or has another mark flown her out for the weekend? And at this point, this relationship is far beyond worth it, but you can't see it yet because you are still blinded by love. This doesn't apply to a pimps and players because they have a few women in rotation anyway. This applies to the simps and the lovers who are all in, hoping and believing that they have a good woman on their side. Sometimes you do have a good woman by your side but you still getting tricked. Good women trick too but godly women do not. Once they become godly, they should reform from their wicked trickin ways. But I hear someone raising that point the church women are tricks too. Yes, church women are tricks too, which is why I said, "GODLY" women. Once she has the Lord on her side and wants to do right, then she might actually develop a little bit care and emotional concern for her mark. But until then, there is no hope my good sir. A trick will be a trick, and you will have to deal the trick accordingly.

The other option that the mark has is to expose the trick or let it ride like you are oblivious to the trickery. If you confront the trick with your suspicious and intuitive belief that she is using you and that she doesn't really love you like she says, just be prepared to be gaslighted. She will convince you that the feeling is in your head and that she loves like no one else on earth. Follow your gut! Do not be swayed by the attempt to keep the trickery going. Self-preservation and maintaining the status quo is important to the trick. No trick wants to lose a loving and faithful mark—that is the best kind of man, one that loves you and wants to provide for you. You don't have to beg when someone wants to give naturally. Someone that wants to see you win will go out of there way to get you the resources to do so. So a good mark is one that no trick wants to loose. Just be prepared for that conversation to not go the way you have planned. A trick is never honest—even when she is telling the truth, she still lying because the motives are not pure. She only in the situation for the bag—she doesn't give a damn about you. No matter how much you want her to be the one—she trickin! She is at work, and you are the paycheck provided.

So either boss up or you will maintain the status quo. Boss up and set new boundaries if you want to keep the trick around. But she does not belong to you, so do not expect the same level of access or engagement because you are no longer providing payment like you used to do. But the trickin will continue as long as you allow it to go on. Start saying "no" and or not providing immediately when she asked and watch how fast the relationship begins to fade. Now if you don't mind being a mark and you just want the benefit of having access to this particular trick—special and extraordinary tricks do exist—then accept that you are paying for her time and continual presence in your soon to be miserable life if you continue to let the trick play with you. At some point you will watch your checking and savings deplete down to zero. You will be on time with her bills and late with your own. The status quo will eventually have you in the poor house and I guarantee that trick will not be there to assist you with any of your problems because she will already on to the next mark. Boss up, boss!

7
END IT!

Just go ahead and end it! The sooner that you end this trick situation, the sooner you will be able to recover. Rejection is hard by itself, but you will make it through. Breaking up with the trick you love is an even worse feeling, but you will recover too. It will hurt—tremendously it will. It will hurt in places that you did not know existed. You will grieve the loss of what you once thought was yours, what you once thought was real love. But the reality is the circus performance has left town, and you will be better off for it. Cease the wicked from troubling your life and allow the healing process to begin. The longer it takes you to end this trickery, the more trials and tribulations you will endure. This may feel like a tragic loss especially to the simps and good men but trust me you will make it through this. This will be one of the best decisions in your life—to end the trickery. You may not see it now, but you will thank yourself up the road of life.

I do understand that walking away and/or being the first person to terminate the relationship is a hard thing to do. It's like you are giving up on the hopes of your dreams—what you are really doing is ending the delusion that you have this trick is the "one" for you. For those with joint accounts and intermingled assets, this will present many challenges. Some of you simps out there have cosigned for vehicles, homes, apartments, property, appliances, the little baby's school tuition—you name it. It will be hard to take your name of the apartment lease five months into the twelve-month lease. The best thing you can do is pray and hope that the new mark will come through for you. Hope and pray that whoever else has been paying those bills for the trick will continue to do when you have left. Do realize that the trick will miss you when you are gone. She will miss those monthly payments and groceries that you faithfully delivered. You will not just slip away unnoticed. The trick will also grieve your loss, but she will be quickly comforted by the new dick that she been sleeping with for the past few weeks.

Once you hit the eject button and beam yourself out of the trickin situation, then it's over. You will never regain the level of security that you enjoyed in the initial stages of your own delusion. The truth of the matter is the trick was never all that. You created a fantasy or idea of her in your mind that you fell in love with. She never checked all the boxes for the one that you really wanted—there is no way that she did because nowhere on your list of ideals were the desires to disrespected, the desire to be cheated on, the desire to be played and used for your money only. It was all a delusion. It was just a world of make-believe that you created in your own mind because saw something that looked good and you didn't want to be alone. The pussy was good while it lasted but another pussy will come along with will feel just like the last one. You have not lost the world when you leave. Life goes on—hurt and broken as you may be—you will get over this. How do I know this? Because although you may be a simp and a blinded lover, you are still a man! Man up and walk boldly in the world. Seek, hunt, and find that Proverbs 31 woman—

a good thing. Good women are out here—godly women are out here seeking a great man to help build their lives together.

End the trickery! End it! Find the courage and the will to end it! Walk away now and do so without apology. Make sure that you have minimized your liabilities and the damage that will happen to your finances, but it is best to end it while you are ahead because it will eventually end. How long will you allow her to play in your because remember that you blocked from her IG story so there is a whole other world of relationships and trickery that she is playing with outside your line of view. Just end it! Be brave! Walk away now! Trickin is not for the weak nor the faint of heart. Trickin can and will destroy you if you let it. Stop helping someone else get their bag. You should be working on your own bag! Get your own bag up and the world will open up to you!

So I leave you with this—it is hard out here for a trick when the simps realize they actually bosses. Trickin is an art, and many women are skilled tricksters. Since the dawn of time, trickin has been here and it will be her until time and earth no longer exists.

ABOUT THE AUTHOR

A'Lisa Ray is a reformed American trick. She was a master
manipulator and is highly skilled in trickology. Thee Stallion was a
protégé of Ray and has mastered the trickin' game.